Text by John Peel

Cover Illustration by Paul Vaccarello

Interior Illustration by John Nez

Western Publishing Company, Inc.,
Racine, Wisconsin 53404

 Library of Congress Catalog Card Number: 91-70569 ISBN: 0-307-22202-0 MCMXCII

Your Briefing

Congratulations — you've been hired as a rookie detective for the Acme Detective Agency. Your goal is to outsmart Carmen Sandiego and her gang by solving the cases in this book. Each time you solve a case and make the least amount of moves, you'll get a promotion.

There are four cases to solve in this book. To solve each case, start by removing the cards from the insert in the middle of this book. Divide the cards into four groups. You should have the following:

4 Bookmark / Scorecards
4 Stolen Object Cards
8 Suspect Cards
8 Map Cards

Use a different ***scorecard*** *for each game to write down clues and eliminate suspects. When you arrive in a new town, use the same card as a* ***bookmark*** *to mark the place that you're in while you're investigating — sometimes you'll have to retrace your steps.*

Each case involves a stolen object. Decide which case you are going to solve by picking a ***stolen object card****. Put the other stolen object* *cards away until you are ready to solve those cases.*

As you read each case you will be given clues about different suspects. Use those clues and the ones on the back of the ***suspect cards*** *to decide which suspect you must capture. When you have made your decision, put the other suspect cards aside. The suspect card you have chosen serves as your warrant for the arrest.*

Use the ***map cards*** *for information on the various places that you'll have to visit while tracking down a suspect. Put aside any cards that don't fit the clues you are given, until you have only one map card left.*

Each time you are told to go to a different number in the story, mark that move point on your scorecard. At the end of each game, add up the total points. Check your score on the last page to see if you've earned a promotion.

Now put on your raincoat, make sure you've got a pen or pencil, and get ready to start your first Acme Detective Agency case.

You're seated in your office in the Acme Detective Agency, staring at the clock on the wall. You've been on the job a full year now, and it's time for your vacation. Boy, have you earned it! Just trying to get that coffee machine in the lounge to work has taken you a full year. You've got your plane tickets for Hawaii, and your bags are packed. You glance at the clock again. Your vacation officially starts today at five o'clock. Good — it's 4:53 — not much longer to wait. . . .

You're just beginning to wonder if you can sneak out early when the phone on your desk rings.

It's the Chief, and he wants to see you right away. You sigh. It sounds like trouble. Maybe you won't be going to Hawaii after all. . . .

When you enter the Chief's office, you can tell how worried he is. As you approach his desk he tosses you a folder. "Sorry about this," he growls. He doesn't sound sorry, just tired. "Unfortunately, you're the best person for the case."

"Yeah?" you ask, opening the file. It's marked "Carmen Sandiego." You know all about her — but isn't she still in jail from the last time you caught her?

Inside the file are eight new faces you've never seen before. You look up at the Chief.

"Carmen's in jail, but eight members of her gang are still on the loose," he tells you. "And I've just gotten word that four national treasures have been stolen. Take your pick where you want to start." He throws you another file.

"Inside this folder are details of the stolen treasures and maps of the places around the U.S.A. that are involved." Then he hands you four separate cards.

"Each time you make a move, mark down your travel points on these cards. You're in line for a promotion, and we'll be using them to grade you when the case is over.

"Get these cases cracked," he promises, "and we'll even give you a bonus — and fly you to Hawaii for free."

Finally the Chief hands you another batch of cards. "These are snapshots of the members of Carmen's gang. Don't forget to get a warrant for the right person before you make an arrest, otherwise the thief will get away with it."

"Don't worry, Chief," you tell him. "I'm sure I'll spot the right clues in order to eliminate the wrong suspects. By the time I find the stolen treasures, I'll have the right robber identified, too."

"Remember, only Carmen's gang would be bold enough to steal these things. So forget your vacation for now and get on the case. I don't care what order you take them in, but I want the stolen treasures back and the guilty parties arrested."

"I got it, Chief," you tell him.

He manages a small smile, and you see he's hoping you'll pull this off.

A bonus and a promotion, eh? Nice! You could always use a little more cash on your vacation. But first you've got to get these mysteries solved. Opening the report, you check out the four stolen objects and the eight suspects. Picking up your note pad and a map of the U.S.A., you try to decide which treasure you'll track down first. You follow the instructions on each card.

If you've chosen to recapture:

The Alamo — go to 34.

The Grand Canyon — go to 140.

The Winslow Homer painting, Gulf Stream — go to 100.

The Golden Gate Bridge — go to 65

1. You've arrived in Des Moines, Iowa. You wish you had time to visit its Capitol Building. The building has a 274-foot gilded dome that is the largest in the country. Sounds like an interesting sight. But as always, it's business before pleasure. The local agent is waiting for you with a good, strong cup of coffee. While you sip it, he gives you his report.

"The guy you're after was definitely seen here," he tells you. "I found out he visited three sights in the state and that he left to go to one of three cities." You check his notes.

If you want to investigate:
The Keokuk Dam, in Iowa — go to 114
Fort Dodge, Iowa — go to 159
The Living History Farms, in Iowa — go to 46

If you're ready to follow your suspect to:
Sacramento, California — go to 21
Augusta, Maine — go to 74
Madison, Wisconsin — go to 127

2. You land in Raleigh, North Carolina. There's no one here to meet you. Puzzled, you look around. You begin to get the horrible suspicion that you're in the wrong place. Better head to 31.

3. The tour guide outside the Salt Lake City Temple, in Utah, greets you. Before you get a chance to say anything, she starts chattering away:

"Right behind us is the Salt Lake City Temple of the Mormon Church. It was dedicated in 1893, and its walls stand 167 feet high.

"The walls were chiseled out of granite from the mountains you can see in the distance. That statue you see on top of the temple is of the angel Moroni. Near the temple is another building called the Tabernacle and it is the home of the world-famous Mormon Tabernacle Choir."

When she pauses to take a breath, you plunge in. "Actually, I'm just looking for the thief of the Winslow Homer painting *Gulf Stream*. I understand you might have seen her." You put the picture in front of her face before she has a chance to say anything else.

"Oh, yes," she replies. "I remember her. She looked at the angel. Then she told me that where she was going next, she'd be checking out something to do with flying."

You thank her and return to 68 to check the possible places the thief might be heading.

4. You arrive at the address you've been given for Miles Long, but he's not here. The place is deserted. There's a short note: Go to 120.

5. The railroad engineer at the Boothbay Railway Village, in Maine, greets you as you arrive. He's been polishing one of the engines, and now it gleams. You admire his work and then ask him about the man you're after.

"Yes, I remember him." The engineer frowns. "Didn't like trains at all. Obviously he has no taste. He told me he was off to some famous lake to go boating. I told him he was crazy. I mean, why spend time on a boat when you can spend it on a train?"

"Right," you agree. It's time for you to get moving. It's back to Augusta, Maine (74) to check out where your man is heading. You wonder if you have time to catch a train. . . .

6. The Okefenokee Swamp is at the junction of the St. Marys and Suwannee rivers. You've heard of the second one — Stephen Foster wrote about it. "Way down upon the Swanee River," you start to sing. One of the national park rangers tells you to stop because your singing is scaring the wildlife.

"Don't they appreciate good music?" you ask him.

"Sure, when they hear some," he snaps back.

"Did you get a chance to hear the man I'm after?" you ask.

"He was an even worse singer than you," the ranger answers. "I threw him out. He said he was going to some other national park, where he would be better appreciated."

You thank the ranger for his help, and as you leave the park you treat him to your version of "Twinkle, Twinkle, Little Star." You hear him screaming for peace as you head back to Atlanta, Georgia (35).

7. The Crater of Diamonds lies just outside of Murfreesboro, Arkansas. It is the only diamond mine ever worked in the United States, and you're not surprised that one of Carmen's gang would head there!

You pull your rented car into the first available parking space. Next to you is a man repairing a flat tire. You go over to help him, but he jumps up and rushes at you. Obviously he's one of Carmen's contacts, lying in wait for you.

"You're too smart, flatfoot," he growls, trying to hit you with his wrench. "But I'll stop you."

Just as he's about to hit you with the wrench he trips over the tire jack and hits his head against your car. He's knocked out cold. When you go through his wallet, you find a list of addresses for the suspects in your case. One of the park rangers sees everything and runs over.

"Is everything all right?" he asks.

"Just hold this man until the police can arrest him," you tell him.

"What happened to him?" the ranger asks.

"Oh, he's just tired," you reply. "Tell the police he's charged with assault."

"What about the pepper?" says the ranger.

This really isn't your day. Instead of answering the ranger, you merely sigh and look over your list.

If you want to arrest:

Polly Esther Fabrique — go to 64
Earl E. Bird —go to 36
Nick Brunch — go to 141
Molly Coddle — go to 165
June Bug — go to 84
Miles Long — go to 116
Dazzle Annie Nonker — go to 157
Mylar Naugahyde — go to 48

8. The Space Needle stands in the Seattle Center, which you get to by riding the monorail running through the heart of the city. You take the elevator to the observation deck six hundred feet up. From there you can clearly see the mountains and Puget Sound. You also see your contact, a tour guide, and ask her what she knows.

"Seattle was founded in 1852, and it expanded during the Alaskan gold rush in 1897," she tells you. "And after —"

"About the woman who stole the Golden Gate Bridge," you say quickly, before she gives you any more facts about the city.

"Oh, her. She kept joking about this being a Space Needle but how she was off to a place where she could see a crater — and it wasn't on the Moon."

You think about this as you head back to Olympia, Washington (101).

9. You've arrived in Olympia, the capital of the state of Washington. It's the gateway to the Olympic Mountains, a great area for skiing. You wish you had time to try out the slopes. You sigh when the local agent arrives dressed warmly and carrying a pair of skis.

"Glad you arrived," he says, grinning. "As soon as I've briefed you, I'm going skiing."

"No kidding," you say with a growl. "I hope you find a nice slope with a lake at the end."

He laughs and hands you the information he's gathered. Three places to check and three towns your thief might have gone to.

If you want to check:

Mount Rainier, in Washington — go to 66

Skid Road, in Seattle — go to 17

The Grand Coulee Dam, in Washington —go to 42

If you think the thief has gone to:
Little Rock, Arkansas —go to 110
Cheyenne, Wyoming —go to 163
Augusta, Maine —go to 98

10. Here you are in Des Moines, Iowa. As you look around, a businessman approaches you and hands you a letter. Inside is a short message: Go to 31.

11. You've arrived at Kitty Hawk, North Carolina. It was on this beach in 1903 that Wilbur and Orville Wright became the first people to fly an airplane. You spot a man flying a kite and go over to talk with him. He makes his kite do a loop-the-loop as he listens to your questions.

"Yeah, I saw the dame you're after," he tells you. "She seemed a bit up in the air about something. She said she was off to a place where she could get some terrific grapes."

You thank him for his help and head back to Raleigh, North Carolina (108), to check your notes.

12. Feeling somewhat foolish, you arrive at

Disneyland, in California. Everywhere you look, there are people walking around dressed as the famous Disney characters. Kids of all ages pass you by, singing snatches of "It's a Small World." One of the Disney characters comes up to you. It's a mouse dressed like Sherlock Holmes. Cute.

"Who are you?" you ask him.

"Why, I'm Basil of Baker Street — at your service!" the mouse replies.

The Great Mouse Detective, eh? Well, you could use some help. You ask about the theft of the Golden Gate Bridge.

"Well," Basil tells you, "aside from the fact that the thief was female and heading for a famous river, I can really tell you nothing."

Hey, this mouse is good! He's obviously no Mickey Mouse detective. You head back to San Francisco, California (65), to get some more clues.

13. When you check the address for Mylar Naugahyde you discover it's a bird sanctuary. There's a small room available for bird-watching called a hide. It figures. Where else would Mylar Naugahyde hide — except in a hide? You'll never know, because he isn't here. There's a message scrawled out in the dust: Go to 120.

14. So this is Baraboo, Wisconsin. According

to your guidebook, this is where the Ringling Bros. Circus got its start. Nowadays, the show's old winter quarters house the Circus World Museum, and you can hear the famous music coming from the buildings. One of the shows is under way. You spot a clown and tap him on the shoulder. He screams, jumps a foot in the air, and falls dramatically to the ground.

"Overacting," you complain.

"Everyone's a critic," he replies. "What do you want, pal?"

You ask him about the thief you're trailing.

"Oh, that joker," the clown replies. "He was feeding peanuts to the elephants. He ran out, saying he was going to a place where he could invest in peanuts."

As you head back to Madison, Wisconsin (99), you check your list to see where the thief might be going.

15. "So this is Sacramento, California," you say to yourself. Well, where is everybody? There's a public telephone nearby, and you call the local office. The secretary is surprised to hear from you.

"What are you doing in Sacramento?" she asks. "The Chief says you'd better get to 31."

16. Augusta, Maine — but there's no one here

to meet you. You call the local office. They don't know why you're in Augusta and suggest that you head to 31.

17. You've come to Skid Road, in Seattle, Washington. In 1852 Henry Yesler built the first steam-powered sawmill at the end of this road, which fronts on Puget Sound. To get the logs to the mill, they were "skidded" down the road.

As Seattle expanded, Skid Road became a depressed area and gave rise to the use of "skid row" to mean the worst place in town.

Nowadays, you notice, it's not bad at all. Town laws have made it into a historic district. You spot a local policeman and ask about the thief you're hunting.

"All I can tell you is that he had piercing brown eyes," the officer says. "And that he was heard saying he was going to a national park."

You thank him and head back to Olympia, Washington (9).

18. You've arrived at a baby-clothes store, which makes sense. Just the sort of place that Molly Coddle would choose as a hideout. But the place is closed. Using your skeleton key, you enter the store. On the cash register is a note. It says: Go to 120.

19. You turn your rented car into the entrance of the Air Force Museum at Wright-Patterson Air Force Base, just outside of Fairborn, Ohio. As you recall, the museum has more than 150 aircraft and spacecraft on display, and more than twenty thousand exhibits in all. Pity you don't have the time to check them out. Instead, you talk to one of the men in uniform and ask about the woman you're tracking.

"Yes, I saw her," the airman replies. "She said something about going mountaineering when she left here."

Thanking him, you head back to Columbus, Ohio (137), to check where she might be headed.

20. The Amana Colonies turn out to be seven Old World villages in Iowa. You read that they were founded by Christian Metz in 1854 for a group of people called the Inspirationalists.

The Inspirationalists started their own factories to build furniture and other household items. Their work turned out to be so good that they are still selling pieces of it to this day. There's a museum, an old house, and plenty of places to eat. Thank goodness! You're starved.

You stop at one restaurant, and while you're enjoying your meal, you ask about the woman you're looking for.

"Oh, I saw her," the waitress tells you. "She ate here, too. She was blond and said she was going off to look for goldfinches. I think she believed they were really made of gold."

"It figures," you tell her, finishing your food. "Carmen's gang would steal anything they think even *sounds* valuable." You leave the waitress a good tip as you head back to Des Moines, Iowa (37), to check on this new information.

21. You arrive in Sacramento, California to find a message from the Chief. "You're in the wrong place," it reads. "Go straight to 31."

22. The Lyndon B. Johnson Space Center in Houston, Texas, is the hub of NASA's space shuttle program. The space center has plenty to see — from moon rocks to training devices used to get astronauts ready for space. You wish you had time to explore it all. But it's business before pleasure, and you ask one of the astronauts about the man you're looking for.

"Yeah, I remember him," she tells you. "Funny guy, eating fried chicken. Said he was going to a famous battlefield from here."

You thank her and head back to Austin, Texas (119), to check the clues.

23. Mount Palomar, California, is home to one of the two Hale Observatories (the other being on Mount Wilson). The huge dome is on the mountaintop and houses a telescope and a two-inch mirror. Until 1973 it was the world's largest telescope. It is still used to gather information about the universe. You hope, however, to get some information a bit closer to home. One of the astronomers proves to be of help.

"Yes, I saw the woman you're looking for," he tells you. "She said she had come to the wrong place and was actually looking for mockingbirds."

Noting this, you head back to Sacramento, California (56).

24. You've arrived in Olympia, the capital of Washington State. To your surprise, there's no one to meet you. You call the local office, and all that they can suggest is that you try going to 31.

25. The tumbleweed drifts across the deserted street of this old Nevada ghost town. Getting out of your car, you look around. The buildings are old and abandoned. You can just imagine John Wayne or Clint Eastwood coming out of the saloon. Wait a minute — someone *is* coming out of the saloon!

It's obviously one of Carmen's gang. He puts his hand on his holster, and you know he plans to shoot you. You dive for cover and think fast. Before the plan is even clear in your mind, you pick up a medium-sized rock. You aim directly at the loose sign over the saloon doors. The rotten wood holding up the sign breaks, and the sign crashes down, knocking out the villain.

You're definitely very close to catching your thief. Better return to Carson City, Nevada (123), and watch your step!

26. You're at the Petrified Forest National Park in the Painted Desert of Arizona. It's quite amazing — trees that died 160 million years ago have been turned to stone, such as jasper and agate. The trees are very beautiful, but eerie. This is just the sort of place that would attract one of Carmen's gang. You ask one of the park rangers about the thief you're after.

"I saw the man you're looking for," the ranger tells you. "He tried to steal one of the trees. But we're very careful that no one could destroy this place by taking even a small sample, let alone a whole tree. He left here in a hurry. I noticed a map showing some canyon or other. Maybe he's going there next."

Considering that this is the thief who stole the Grand Canyon, you figure he's got a thing about canyons. Well, it's back to Flagstaff, Arizona (140).

27. Roanoke Island, just off the coast of North Carolina, was the first English settlement in America. It was founded by John White in 1587. It is also the place of one of the great mysteries of history: When White returned to the island from a trip to England in 1590, all 117 of the settlers had vanished. Weird! But you're after someone who has been known to vanish.

You ask one of the local fisherman for information. "Oh, I saw her all right," he tells you. "Funny-looking thing with bright brown eyes. Seemed quite silly to me."

Making a note of his information, you return to Raleigh, North Carolina (108).

28. You arrive at a tall, stately mansion on the outskirts of Atlanta, Georgia, but it's obviously

been closed for years. The "For Sale" sign is swinging in the wind. You check out the place, but it's clear that if Earl E. Bird was ever here, he has long since flown the coop. With a sigh, you head for 120.

29. As you look up at Devils Tower National Monument, in Wyoming, you can't get over the feeling that you've seen it somewhere before. Spooky! Looking at your guidebook, you discover that it was the country's first national monument, established in 1906.

Devils Tower is a mass of volcanic rock, one thousand feet wide at the bottom and narrowing to 275 feet wide at the top. It looks like something from another world — now you remember where you saw it. It's where Steven Spielberg filmed *Close Encounters of the Third Kind*!

You talk to one of the park rangers, and she grins. "Yes, I saw the man you're looking for," she tells you. "He mentioned that he was going to see a famous river after this."

Thanking her, you head back to Cheyenne, Wyoming (163), wondering which river the thief might have gone to.

30. Crystal Falls Cave, Idaho, is only one of many caves that tourists can visit in Idaho. There

are also the Mammoth Cave and the Shoshone Ice Caves. Caves don't really light up your life, even with the glittering icicle-like stalactites and stalagmites they contain.

You talk to the girl at the ticket office, and she nods. "Yes, I remember him. He had blond hair and said he was going after corn."

Glad to be back out in the open skies you return to Boise, Idaho (55), to add up your clues.

31. Well, it's time to face facts. You've messed up somewhere along the way. The trail of the crook you're after has gone cold. Better return to the last city you were in and check your facts again. You did remember to keep your place marked, didn't you?

32. This is Austin, Texas, where everything is big, including mistakes. Boy, have you made a whopper! You're in the wrong place. Go to 31. Don't worry, it's very close!

33. You've been in some odd places in your life, but this has to be one of the strangest! The Underground Tours take you below the city streets of Seattle. In the odd light, you see preserved shops and buildings and even the old level of the street.

When the city was rebuilt, the road here was raised to the level of the second story, leaving the old levels in place — and underground.

You talk to the tour guide to see if the woman you're after has been here. He shrugs.

"We get lots of people down here," he tells you. "Some of them are even crazier than you."

Muttering mean thoughts under your breath, you head back to Olympia, Washington (101).

34. Your plane lands in San Antonio, Texas. There to meet you is the local agent, a friendly young woman with long, blond hair and freckles that seem to light up when she welcomes you.

"Been doing plenty of research for you," she says, handing you a list. "This dude you're after made a big mistake when he stole the Alamo. Folks here will never forget him. You shouldn't have much trouble picking up his trail."

You look over her work and congratulate her on her efficiency.

If you want to investigate:

Laredo, Texas — go to 102

Abilene, Texas — go to 143

Dallas, Texas — go to 167

If you've discovered the thief is in:

Des Moines, Iowa — go to 50

Olympia, Washington —go to 9
Austin, Texas —go to 78

35. As you get off the plane in Atlanta, Georgia, the heat hits you like a hammer. You're happy to see the agent from the local office pull up in his car. You get in, and as you settle back in air-conditioned comfort, you frown as he grins.

"If you think the weather's hot, wait until you see the tips I've got for you!"

After you groan at his attempt at a joke, you look at the list.

If you want to investigate:
Six Flags Over Georgia —go to 71
Savannah, Georgia —go to 95
Okefenokee Swamp, in Georgia —go to 6

If you're ready to chase the crook to:
Carson City, Nevada —go to 47
Austin, Texas —go to 119
Little Rock, Arkansas —go to160

36. You've tracked Earl E. Bird deep into the Ozark Mountains, in Arkansas, but there's no sign of him now. Feeling lost and bewildered, you realize you must head for 120.

37. You arrive in Des Moines, Iowa, and the

local agent greets you. You like the city, and you like the smiling young man who hands you a list.

"The woman you're after definitely stopped here, but she's already left," he tells you. "I've found three places for you to check and noted the only three towns she could have gone to."

If you want to look into:
The Amana Colonies, in Iowa — go to 20
Le Claire, Iowa — go to 73
The Salisbury House, in Iowa — go to 142

But if you're ready to travel to:
Olympia, Washington — go to 101
Atlanta, Georgia — go to 154
Boise, Idaho — go to 49

38. This is one Nevada ghost town that's *completely* empty. There's no sign of Dazzle Annie Nonker here, so you head to 120.

39. Little Rock, Arkansas, seems like a nice place, but there's no one here from the local office. When you call, you're told that you have to travel on to 31.

40. The Metroparks Zoo in Cleveland, Ohio, is a sprawling place where many of the animals live out in the open, instead of in cages. You love zoos,

and you wish you had time to visit all the animals. With a sigh, you get back to work and approach one of the zoo keepers.

"Yes, I remember the woman you're looking for," she replies. "She mentioned she was going to pick soybeans next."

Thanking the zoo keeper, you decide to return to Columbus, Ohio (137), to investigate more clues.

41. Meteor Crater (also known as Barringer Crater), in Arizona, is a strange hole in the ground. It is 580 feet deep and 4,100 feet wide. The crater was discovered in 1891 and is believed to have been caused by a two-million-ton meteor hitting the earth in prehistoric times. A staggering thought!

You approach one of the tourists and ask him about the woman you're looking for.

"Oh, yeah," he replies. "I know the one you mean. She said she was off to a national park, and then she hightailed it out of here. Not long ago. You should find her soon, I guess."

Thanking him, you return to Phoenix, Arizona (85), to check out the clues.

42. The Grand Coulee Dam is situated on the Columbia River. It's located in the state of Washington, and stands 550 feet high and 4,173

across — quite an impressive structure. The dam is used to irrigate two thousand square miles of farmland. It took eight years to build — from 1933 to 1941. Behind the dam is a 151-mile-long lake.

Well, you're not here to sit and look at the dam. You approach one of the workers and ask him about the man you're after.

"I saw him," the worker tells you. "He had narrow brown eyes, and he mentioned he was going to do some mining after this."

You thank the man, and head back to Olympia, Washington (9), to investigate these latest clues.

43. You arrive at the Lewis and Clark Cavern, in Montana, but the attraction is closed for the day and no one is here. If Miles Long was ever here, he's long gone by now. You head for 120.

44. York Village, in Maine, is a historic site that contains a number of beautifully restored old houses, some dating back as far as 1720. You wander around, looking at some of the interesting sights, such as an old jail and an old warehouse. Then you remember you're not here to play tourist! You stop one of the workers to ask about the woman you're after.

"Yes, I remember her," he tells you. "She said she was going to a more modern place; one that had electronics." He smiles.

You thank him and head back to Rockland, Maine (100), to check on the clue he gave you.

45. Yellowstone National Park, in Wyoming, is immense and may be one of the most beautiful places on Earth. You stop in the area that has geysers — vast jets that erupt out of spout holes. The most famous of these geysers, Old Faithful, erupts every hour and has done so for the last eighty years. Still, it's time for business, not sightseeing, so you talk to a ranger.

He remembers the thief you're after. "She had deep green eyes," he tells you. "Really lovely. And she said she was going to go peanut picking after this."

You thank him, just as Old Faithful erupts . The five-minute burst sprays ten thousand gallons of boiling water over one hundred feet into the air. You head back to Cheyenne, Wyoming (158), to make a note of the clues.

46. Living History Farms, in Iowa, is in fact a reconstructed pioneer village. It's actually made up of three different farms. There's the Pioneer Farm, which shows how farmwork was done in 1840. Then there's Horse-Powered Farm, showing how farmwork was done in 1900. Finally there's

the Farm of Today and Tomorrow, which shows present-day farming methods and farming methods that may be used in the future.

You talk to one of the farmers, and he remembers seeing the man you're after.

"He said he'd had enough of farming and was going to check out a museum that was dedicated to some form of transport or other."

As you head back to Des Moines, Iowa (1), you consider where the thief may be headed.

47. Carson City, Nevada, seems to be out in the middle of nowhere, and you soon discover that that is exactly where you are: nowhere. There's no one waiting for you, so you head to 31.

48. You look around for Mylar Naugahyde, but there's neither hide nor hair of him. Realizing that you've made a bad mistake, you pluck up your courage and head off to 120.

49. Boise, Idaho, is the capital of the Gem State, and you've made a beauty of a mistake here. There's no sign of anyone waiting for you. When you call the local office, they tell you to get yourself over to 31 immediately.

50. It seems very quiet in Des Moines, Iowa, so

you stop at a local bar to call the office. "Where's the man who should have met me?" you complain.

"Where you *should* be," the secretary snaps back. "He went to 31."

51. Charles Russell was one of the greatest cowboy artists who ever lived. You go into his studio-turned-museum in Great Falls, Montana, and see a guy in cowboy clothes trying to rob the place. Quickly you grab one of the ropes off the wall and throw it.

Perfect! The noose slips over his head, and you reel him in. Kicking and screaming, he suddenly recognizes you.

"Darn!" he exclaims. "I was supposed to wait and git you, but I couldn't resist tryin' to steal a paintin' — they're so good."

"Then I'd advise you not to resist arrest, either," you tell him. As the police take him away, you realize that you must be getting very close to the thief you're after! Back to Helena, Montana (132), to try again!

52. Austin is the capital of Texas, the Lone Star State. And right now you're very alone. Puzzled, you call the local office. "They're all out on cases," the secretary tells you. "Maybe you'd better try going to 31."

53. The Fernbank Science Center, in Atlanta, Georgia, is a fascinating place that is filled with all kinds of working models and displays. It contains the third largest planetarium in the country. Maybe, if you get this case solved quickly, you'll have time to stop by and see the show.

"You like stars?" one of the other tourists asks you.

"I love them," you answer.

With a snarl, he pulls a blackjack out of his pocket. "I'll help you to see some stars, pal!" he says as he lunges at you. Quickly you stick out your leg and trip him. Then you grab him in a judo hold and throw him over your shoulder. He sails through the air and lands face down in a garbage can.

"Well, he knows where he belongs," you tell the police when they arrive. "In with the other trash. Book him, guys."

As you think about how close you must be to the thief you're after, you head back to Atlanta, Georgia (122), to check out another lead.

54. You've traveled a lot of miles looking for Miles Long, and it's clear that he just isn't here. It's time for you to head for 120.

55. Boise, Idaho, is the gateway to some of the most spectacular scenery in all of America. It has

lakes, waterfalls, caves, mountains, and miles and miles of forest. As you browse through the guide-book, a young woman from the local office arrives.

"I've rented a car for you ," she tells you, handing over the keys and a list. "I've also tracked down a few places your thief may have gone to." You thank her and look at the list:

To investigate:
Crystal Falls Cave, Idaho — go to 30
The Craters of the Moon, Idaho — go to 111
Shoshone Falls, Idaho — go to 63

If you're ready to leave for:
Madison, Wisconsin — go to 99
Des Moines, Iowa — go to 10
Augusta, Georgia — go to 148

56. Your plane has landed in Sacramento, California. Almost back home again — the Acme Detective Agency is just down the state from here. You think about your Hawaii vacation and shake your head. Once the job's over, you can think about vacation travel again. Right now you've got to concentrate on the case.

There's no one here to meet you, but there is a note for you to call the office. When you do, your secretary answers.

"I have some information to give you over the

phone," she tells you. "Get ready to take it down."

"Where's the local agent?" you ask her.

"He's gone on vacation," she replies. "After all, he's done his work."

"Doesn't seem fair that he can take off and I can't," you mutter to yourself. Oh, well, it's all part of the job. You take down the information she gives you.

If you want to look for clues in:
Mount Palomar, California — go to 23
The La Brea Tar Pits, in California — go to 145
Hollywood, California — go to 76

If you're ready to depart for:
Austin, Texas — go to 52
Little Rock, Arkansas — go to 161
Carson City, Nevada — go to 125

57. You approach Mount St. Helens a little uneasily. After all, this is a real, live volcano. It erupted in 1980, after 123 years of peace, and no one really knows when it just might decide to erupt again. You hope that it's not while you're around. There's still smoke rising from the ground, and you ask a state trooper how safe it is.

"Oh, the ground's perfectly safe," he answers, with a straight face. "But I wouldn't hang around the volcano if I were you."

Ummm, everyone wants to be a comedian. You ask the trooper if he's seen the woman you're searching for. He nods.

"Yeah. She said this place was too unstable for her. She was heading to where people can go mining without having to worry about being boiled in lava."

You can sympathize with that! Thanking the man, you head back to Olympia, Washington (101), just as fast as you can!

58. You're in Salt Lake City, Utah, which is built near the shores of the Great Salt Lake. The salty water's not the only thing that tastes bitter right now — so does your mouth. You're all alone, but there's a message for you to head straight to 31.

59. Raleigh, North Carolina, is named for Sir Walter Raleigh, the English explorer who introduced the potato to Europe. You could do with his help now, because you've just discovered that you shouldn't be here. You head for 31.

60. You look around the wasteland of the Dinosaur National Monument, and you're amazed to learn that more dinosaur bones have been discovered on this site than anywhere else in the

country. You even discover that scientists have been able to dig entire dinosaur skeletons out of the ground at one time! There's a museum that displays some of them. If you had more time, you could spend hours here. But you've got to get this job done. Reluctantly you turn away from the museum to question one of the staff.

"Yes, I saw the woman you're after. She stopped by on her way out of the state. Said something about going to look for cardinals."

You head back to Salt Lake City, Utah (68), to think that one over.

61. The Andersonville National Historical Site, in Georgia, is where the infamous Confederate prison stood during the Civil War. This isn't where you'd expect to find one of Carmen's gang — they like to avoid prisons whenever possible! Mylar Naugahyde is nowhere to be seen. You head for 120.

62. Madison, Wisconsin, seems like a nice town, but it's the wrong one for you. You receive a message telling you to head directly to 31.

63. You stand at the top of Shoshone Falls, Idaho, speechless at the sight. Here the Snake River goes over a horseshoe-shaped cliff that's

1,000 feet wide and 212 feet straight down. The noise of the water is deafening, and the spray kicks up like rain. Moving back so you can talk, you ask one of the guides about the thief you're after.

"Blond-haired fellow?" he says. "Oh, he was here, all right. Told me he was going to some state to do some bird-watching. I can't remember what bird, but I know it had a one-word name."

You thank him for his help and head back to Boise, Idaho (55), to complete your notes.

64. You've tracked Polly Esther Fabrique to Hot Springs National Park, in Arkansas. What a great place — not only is it a national park but there're lots of mineral springs here and it's a great place to soak and relax.

Suddenly you spot Polly coming out of one of the buildings. You notice that she's carrying a package under one arm. You creep up quietly behind her and snap a handcuff over the wrist of her free hand. Taken by surprise, she drops the package, and you're able to handcuff both her wrists together.

You pick up the package and carefully unwrap it. Sure enough, it's *Gulf Stream*, the stolen Winslow Homer painting!

"You should know better, Polly," you tell her. "The only way to take a picture honestly is with a camera."

"Let me go, gumshoe," she begs you. "I'll give you $5,000 to forget you ever saw me."

You shake your head in surprise. She's trying to buy you off! "Polly, you're a cracker," you say with a grin.

The police arrive, and you hand over Polly Esther Fabrique and the painting to them. Then you call the Chief.

"Well done," he says happily. "There'll be a promotion in this for sure. And those tickets for Hawaii are waiting on your desk."

It's about time. But before you go on that hard-earned vacation, you'd better head to the back of the book and check your score to see how well you did!

65. San Francisco, California, is one place where you don't need a local agent to do the digging for you. You go to where the Golden Gate Bridge used to stand and start asking questions. In a short while you've got a handful of notes. You put them in order and discover that there are three leads to follow up and three possible places where your thief might have gone.

If you want to investigate:

Yosemite National Park, in California
—go to 89

Disneyland, in California — go to 12
Sequoia National Park, in California — go to 105

If you're ready to leave for:
Carson City, Nevada — go to 130
Atlanta, Georgia — go to 170
Des Moines, Iowa — go to 37

66. Mount Rainier is the highest mountain in Washington State. It is actually a dormant volcano that stands 14,410 feet tall. Except for the mountains of Alaska, Mount Rainier has more glaciers on it than any other mountain in the United States. The largest glacier is on Mount Rainier, however, and it's called Emmons Glacier.

As you arrive at the mountain, you see that plenty of hikers, skiers, and climbers have beaten you to it. You stop one of them to ask about the man you're after. By a stroke of good luck, you picked the right person.

"He said something about going mining," the tourist tells you. "He seemed upset that he couldn't find a mine around here."

"Sounds like one of Carmen's gang," you agree. "Whatever they see, it's all mine, mine, mine."

You head back to Olympia, Washington (9), to decide what to do next.

67. There's no sign at all of June Bug when you arrive in the mining town of Butte, Montana. You realize that you must have made a mistake somewhere and head off with a heavy heart to 120.

68. Salt Lake City, Utah, was built in 1847 near the shore of the Great Salt Lake by Mormons, under the leadership of Brigham Young. It is the world headquarters of the Church of Jesus Christ of Latter-day Saints, the official name for the Mormon Church. Salt Lake City is a prosperous, pleasant city with plenty to see.

The local agent greets you and hands over a list of possibilities for you to look into.

If you want to investigate:
Zion National Park, in Utah —go to 88
The Salt Lake City Temple, in Utah — go to 3
Dinosaur National Monument, in Utah —go to 60

If you are ready to leave for:
Columbus, Ohio —go to 137
Raleigh, North Carolina —go to 169
Austin, Texas —go to 32

69. The Hohokam Native Americans were a tribe of Navajo Indians who lived in Arizona six hundred years ago and left behind some astonish-

ing artifacts.

Many of these remains can be found at the Navajo National Monument, such as the Betatakin Ruin. The ruin looks like a huge prehistoric apartment house. It contains at least 135 rooms and is perched on top of Segi Canyon. The edge of a cliff, however, is not your idea of a fun place to live!

You question one of the local Navajo, and he remembers seeing the woman you're after.

"She was very interested in sightseeing," he tells you. "She mentioned that she'd be going to a national park from here."

You figure she's probably looking for something else to steal. Thanking him for his help, you head back to Phoenix, Arizona (85).

70. Las Vegas, Nevada, with all of its gambling and nightlife, seems like an ideal place for one of Carmen's gang to hang out, but there's no sign at all of June Bug. It looks as if the gang has tricked you. With a sinking feeling, you head for 120.

71. Just as you suspected, Six Flags Over Georgia, near Atlanta, turns out to be an amusement park. There are two super-scary roller-coaster rides, including the Mind-Bender, which has a triple loop. It makes you shudder. In this line of

business you know you have to take chances, but you can't believe anyone would go on a ride like that for fun!

Wondering how the place got its name, you ask one of the ice-cream sellers about it. She smiles.

"It celebrates the six flags that have flown over the state," she explains. "French, Spanish, British, Confederate, the United States — and Georgia's own state flag."

Since she's so helpful, you ask her about the man you're trailing. Again, she knows something.

"He said the roller coaster gave him an appetite to go and see something to do with space."

You think to yourself that the thief had plenty of space, and it was all between his ears. Still, you thank the woman and head back to Atlanta, Georgia (35), to consider this clue.

72. Little Rock, Arkansas, holds very little for you — except a message from the Chief. "What are you doing there?" it reads. "Get to 31 right away."

73. You look around Le Claire, Iowa, the birthplace of Buffalo Bill Cody. Here you find a museum dedicated to his life, including his Wild West Show and to the Native Americans that he both fought

against and respected. The museum has all kinds of marvels from the Old West. There's even a stern-wheel paddleboat restored to its former glory. Walking around the museum is almost like being in the Old West yourself.

You talk to one of the museum curators, and he remembers the woman you're trailing.

"Blond- haired, pretty thing." He sighs. "Shame she's a crook."

"Yeah," you agree. "Pity all crooks don't look like they've been hit by a truck. It'd make them easier to spot. Did she give you any idea where she was going next?"

"She said she was going someplace to climb mountains."

You leave him thinking about the pretty crook and head back to Des Moines, Iowa (37), to add up your clues.

74. So this is Augusta, Maine. You look around while you wait for your contact to arrive. Maine is one of the prettiest New England states. It has plenty of coastline and islands to explore — if you had the time. But right now you've got to nab that thief.

The local agent arrives and apologizes for the delay. "I've been tracking down one last clue," he explains. "I wanted you to have everything you'd need." He hands you a list, and you look it over.

If you want to check:

Acadia National Park, in Maine —go to 82
Rockland, Maine —go to 151
Boothbay Railway Village, in Maine —go to 5

If you're ready to leave for:

Atlanta, Georgia —go to 135
Salt Lake City, Utah —go to 58
Carson City, Nevada —go to 123

75. Cheyenne, Wyoming, was once a rip-roaring, gun-shooting, whiskey-drinking town, but it's peaceful now. So peaceful, in fact, that it doesn't take you long to realize that you've been led astray. You head for 31.

76. You look around in amazement. You're in Hollywood, California, movie capital of the world! You wish you could take a look inside Universal Studios or one of the major television studios. Maybe you have time to see the filming of a movie or the taping of a TV show. . . . Or perhaps to stroll down to Mann's Chinese Theater, where so many movie personalities have made handprints or footprints in the concrete. But you don't have the time — sigh, duty calls.

You approach the doorman at Mann's and ask

him if he's seen the woman you're after.

"She was here," he tells you. "Wanted to know if she could leave her own handprints for the tourists. I told her to clear off, or we'd preserve *all* of her in concrete. She said she'd had enough of these movie-star types and was going to a place where there are plenty of trees."

You head back to Sacramento, California (56), making a note of the latest clue.

77. The Grand Teton Mountains, in Wyoming, are an impressive sight. There's a lot to do in this scenic area — from hiking, to horseback riding, to white-water rafting, to just sitting back and admiring the breathtaking views.

You make a mental note to add this spot to your vacation list. Finally you ask one of the rangers about the woman you're looking for.

"Yes, I remember her. She had green eyes and was interested in bird-watching. I forget the name of the bird she was looking for. I know it had a color in its name, but I can't recall which color."

You head back to Cheyenne, Wyoming (158), to check out more clues.

78. Austin, Texas — but you get a feeling you're in the wrong place. You call the local office.

The secretary there says she had no idea that you were going to be in town and tells you that you had better get along to 31.

79. You've tracked Polly Esther Fabrique to White Sulphur Springs, Montana just outside of Helena, but the trail has run cold. There's no sign of Polly anywhere. Well, there's nothing for you to do now except to head for 120.

80. The tourist spot of Asheville, North Carolina, lies close to the Great Smoky Mountains National Park. It is possible to buy samples of over three hundred varieties of minerals and gems in the local mines.

Asheville is also the town where writers Thomas Wolfe and O. Henry are buried. But you're looking for someone who's still alive, so you go and talk to one of the area 's Cherokee Native Americans.

"I saw the brown-eyed woman around here," he tells you after looking at a photograph. "She said that from here she was going to a place where she could play all day."

You thank him and head back to Raleigh, North Carolina (108), to log that clue.

81. Jekyll Island, Georgia, was once the home

of local millionaires. Now it's a vacation paradise, with long, golden beaches and four golf courses. You arrive at one of these golf courses, looking for your informant.

He's out on the golf course. When he sees you, he begins throwing golf balls at you. He's obviously a member of Carmen's gang. You dodge the golf balls and take cover in a sand trap. Thinking fast, you pick up a nearby golf club. You poke your head out of the sand trap just long enough to hit a golf ball right back at the bad guy.

The ball hits him squarely in the forehead and with a shocked cry, he falls to the ground.

"A hole in one!" you exclaim, and rush over to the dazed thief. You throw him into his golf cart and drive back to the clubhouse to call the police.

You're obviously getting very close now! Back to Atlanta, Georgia (122), to check out the other informants!

82. Acadia National Park, in Maine, combines the mountains and the sea. You stand on top of

Cadillac Mountain and gaze out at the view. The calm waters of the Atlantic and dozens of tiny offshore islands seem so peaceful. But you know the calm could be broken at any moment by one of Carmen's gang. You ask the local inhabitants about the man you're after. Finally, you find a bird-watcher who remembers seeing him.

"Yes, he was here," says the woman. "He told me he was very bored. I suggested he get a pair of binoculars and join me to look for ospreys and bald eagles. He just laughed rudely and said he was going where he could play cards, win some money, and date some cool chicks. What an obnoxious man. I hope you catch him."

"So do I, ma'am," you assure her. You head back to Augusta, Maine (74), to check out the clue she gave you.

83. You've trailed Nick Brunch to a seedy diner on the edge of town. Some of the customers look as if they've been taking ugly lessons. The waitress asks what you're after.

"Brunch," you tell her.

"You're too late for that," she replies. "We only serve brunch on Sundays."

"I don't mean brunch to eat," you say patiently. "I mean Nick Brunch, one of Carmen Sandiego's gang."

"Yeah, that's just who *I* mean," the waitress says with even more patience. "Nick Brunch only comes in on Sundays. And today is Tuesday. You're out of luck, gumshoe."

With a sigh, you head off to 120.

84. You arrive at the Arkansas Alligator Farm, just outside of Hot Springs, Arkansas. So this is where June Bug is supposed to hide out? You soon realize that you're in the wrong place. All you can see for miles around are alligators, and you don't like the way they're smiling at you. You decide to head to 120 before it's feeding time!

85. Your plane lands in Phoenix, Arizona. Your guidebook tells you that this is a terrific place for a vacation. If only you were here for pleasure instead of business. Oh, well, the local agent greets you. She's brought a list for you to look over. You're pleased that she's done such a great job, and you tell her so. Then you read what she's dug up for you.

If you want to investigate:

Meteor Crater, Arizona — go to 41

Navajo National Monument, in Arizona — go to 69

Tucson, Arizona — go to 117

If you've deduced that the crook is in:
Augusta, Maine —go to 16
Helena, Montana —go to 93
Cheyenne, Wyoming —go to 158

86. The circus is inside one of the hotels. As you walk through, you see the live-wire acts, trained animals, and of course the clowns! There are hundreds of children here, so you can see why Molly Coddle might like it. But Molly Coddle is not here. Realizing that you've made a mistake, you pack your things and head for 120.

87. You stand in the town of Tombstone, Arizona, and gaze around you. Once Wyatt Earp and his brothers stood here against the Clanton gang at the famous gunfight at the OK Corral. The corral is still here, along with Boot Hill, where most of the victims of the gunfight are buried.

Another famous attraction is the Wells Fargo office, which was often the target of robbers. Things haven't changed much — there are still crooks lurking around, though you doubt that the man you're after will be wearing a six-gun and waiting for you to shoot it out in the dust.

You ask the clerk in the Wells Fargo Building about the thief.

"He was here," the man tells you. "Said he was going off to a state that had a colorful bird as its emblem."

You thank him and head back to Flagstaff, Arizona (140), to check out the information.

88. Zion National Park, in Utah, is a rich wonderland of rock — from flat-top mesas and canyons to spindly towers of rock that look as though they might collapse at any moment. The park is also filled with flowers. The oddest flower is the two-foot-tall moonflower, which closes in the daytime and opens at night.

You walk up to the botanist who is examining the flower, and start talking about the thief. She recalls the woman you're after.

"I showed her the moonflower, and she wasn't impressed," the botanist tells you. "She said she was much more interested in birds, cardinals in particular. Some people have no taste, do they?"

You couldn't agree more. You head back to Salt Lake City, Utah (68), to think about the latest information.

89. Yosemite Valley, in California, is seven miles long and filled with huge trees, spectacular waterfalls, and strange rock formations. The entire place is breathtakingly beautiful. When

you mention this to one of the guides, he laughs and tells you to come back at Christmastime.

"It's our most popular time," he adds. "Snow, Old World festivities, and a lot of fun. But you have to book over a year in advance. I told this to the woman you're after, and she went off in a bad mood. She didn't want to wait."

"Do you know where she went?" you ask.

"She said something about looking for corn," the guide replies.

You thank him and head back to San Francisco, California (65), to check out your lead.

90. You discover that Cody, Wyoming, is named after Buffalo Bill Cody, the famous Western scout. Preserved in the town are his boyhood home and a very fine museum. The museum contains a huge collection of Winchester rifles, firearms that helped open up the Old West. You feel as though you're about to step into a Clint Eastwood movie.

You talk to the museum curator, and he remembers the man you're after. "He was in here trying to steal some of the old guns. They're pretty valuable, you know."

"Maybe he wants them for his historical collection," you answer. "He's already got the Alamo."

"Anyway, he escaped before I could grab him," the curator adds. "As he sped away, I saw an advertisement in his car for a river trip. I hope that'll help you to track him down."

"It sure will," you tell him. You head back to Cheyenne, Wyoming (163), noting this clue.

91. The Custer Battlefield National Monument at Little Big Horn, Montana, is the site of the infamous Custer's Last Stand. Hot-headed General Custer attacked a huge party of Native Americans, who wiped out his command to the very last man.

While looking around, you spot a man reaching for a bow and arrow that are on display.

"Hey!" you yell and rush over to stop the thief. Hold on! He's pointing the arrow at you! It makes you so mad that before you know it, you've pulled back your fist and punched the guy right between the eyes. With a dazed expression, he collapses. "It's not *my last stand*," you growl at the thief. The guards arrive to cart the man off. As they drag him away, you spot a piece of paper in the back of his shoe.

"Hold it, guys," you call, and you pull out the paper. It's a list of where Carmen's gang is hiding! You're really in luck now.

If you're after:

Nick Brunch — go to 83

Molly Coddle — go to 18

Polly Esther Fabrique — go to 79

Miles Long — go to 43
Mylar Naugahyde — go to 152
Dazzle Annie Nonker — go to 128
June Bug — go to 67
Earl E. Bird — go to 103

92. Eagle Island, Maine, was the home of Admiral Robert Edwin Peary. In 1909 Peary was the first man to reach the North Pole. His house is now preserved and open to visitors.

The guide at the door remembers the woman you're after. "A brown-haired lady, right?" he asks. "Well, as she was leaving she said she was going to explore a famous canyon."

You thank him and head back to Rockland, Maine (100), to investigate more clues.

93. You've arrived in Helena, Montana. It's a nice town, but there's no one here to meet you. Puzzled, you call the local office. There's a message waiting for you from the Chief. It tells you to head straight for 31.

94. "Glitter Gulch," Nevada, is a section of Las Vegas that's away from the major casinos. You enter a hotel and spot the man you're after. He's playing blackjack, and judging from the chips in front of him, he seems to be doing pretty well.

Luckily, he doesn't see you, but gives a nod to the dealer. "Hit me," he says, calling for another card. You can't resist the invitation. You take your notebook and hit him. The thief collapses on the blackjack table, scattering chips everywhere.

Suddenly some cards fall out of his sleeve.

"He had several aces in the hole," you say with a smile. Then you see that one card has writing on it. It's a list of addresses for Carmen's gang! Your luck is running high tonight!

If you're hunting for:

Miles Long — go to 54

Molly Coddle — go to 86

Nick Brunch — go to 118

Polly Esther Fabrique — go to 155

Earl E. Bird — go to 139

June Bug — go to 70

Mylar Naugahyde — go to 13

Dazzle Annie Nonker — go to 38

95. Savannah, Georgia, in the spring is a beautiful sight! The azaleas and dogwoods are in blossom all over the city. Old historic houses abound, and the cotton warehouses have been turned into restaurants, shops, and taverns.

"If you think this is something," one of the shopkeepers tells you, "then you should come back on St. Patrick's Day, when we hold one of the biggest and best festivals in the country!"

You ask the shopkeeper about the man you're after.

"He was in here," the man tells you. "He wanted a book on birds. Said he was looking for a good place to see a mockingbird."

You thank the man and head back to Atlanta, Georgia (35), making note of this.

96. You stand in Grand Prarie, Arkansas, amazed at what you see. Rice is growing in flooded fields the same way it's grown in the paddy fields of China. Yet you're still in the U.S.A.! The farmer notices your expression and laughs.

"If something works, it works," he tells you. "We grow plenty of rice in these parts, and this is the best way to do it."

"Fascinating. What else do you grow around here?" you ask.

"Why, catfish, of course," he replies. Suddenly you spot someone fishing in the field. "Is that allowed?" you ask, pointing.

The farmer is furious. "A catfish burglar!" he howls, running off to fetch his gun. You decide to deal with this thief yourself. To your surprise it's a member of Carmen's gang. He tries to hook you with his fishing rod, but you duck, swing around, and give a judo chop to the neck. He falls backward into the water. Grabbing his shirt, you haul him out.

"It's jail for you," you promise the dripping crook. You head back to Little Rock, Arkansas (161), to fish for some more information.

97. You've trailed Nick Brunch to CNN Plaza in Atlanta, Georgia. It's the headquarters of Cable News Network. But this time around, the news for you is bad — you've followed a cold set of clues. It's not time for Brunch. Better head to 120 instead.

98. You're in Augusta, Maine, but there's no one here to meet you. Puzzled, you buy a local

paper and check out the personals column — one way the Chief can always contact you. There's a brief message there for you: Go to 31.

99. As you drive into Madison, Wisconsin, you are impressed by the beautiful countryside along the river. The town is on a peninsula dotted with many lakes. It's really beautiful, and if you weren't on a case, you might just stop and have a picnic by the river. Oh, well. You drive over to the State Capitol, which is an impressive domed building, where you meet your local contact.

He's brought you a short list of places to check out and possible places that the man you're after may have gone to.

If you want to look into:
Madeline Island, Wisconsin — go to 124
Milwaukee, Wisconsin — go to 168
Circus World Museum, in Baraboo, Wisconsin — go to 14

If you want to trail your thief to:
Raleigh, North Carolina — go to 59
Cheyenne, Wyoming — go to 136
Atlanta, Georgia — go to 35

100. As you drive into Rockland, Maine, you see that it's still a very active fishing port. You

head for the William A. Farnsworth Museum. The local agent, a bright young woman, is waiting for you.

"This thief knew what she was doing," the agent tells you. "She stole one of the painter's most famous paintings, called *Gulf Stream*. Luckily, the museum has other fine Winslow Homer paintings and there are some nice ones by Andrew Wyeth, too."

"I prefer Walt Disney myself," you tell her. "Did you pick up any leads?"

"Three," she says, handing you a list. "And three possible places the thief may have gone to."

If you want to look for clues in:
York Village, Maine — go to 44
Eagle Island, Maine — go to 92
Camden, Maine — go to 121

If you're on the trail of the thief for:
Sacramento, California — go to 15
Salt Lake City, Utah — go to 68
Boise, Idaho — go to 112

101. Your plane touches down in Olympia, Washington, and you're very impressed. On the plane, you saw mountains, huge forests, and many lakes. The state of Washington is a paradise for vacationers. You wish you were one of them.

The local agent greets you at the airport and hands you car keys and a list. “I’ve been pretty busy,” he tells you. “There’re three places where the thief was spotted and three towns that she might have gone to.”

While you check out the list, you decide to have something to drink. Fresh mountain water seems like a good choice, and you start to feel halfway human again.

If you want to check out:

The Underground World, in Seattle, Washington —go to 33
Mount St. Helens, in Washington —go to 57
The Seattle Space Needle, in Washington —go to 8

If you’re ready to move on to:

Phoenix, Arizona —go to 85
Little Rock, Arkansas —go to 166
Cheyenne, Wyoming —go to 134

102. Laredo, Texas, is a bright, cheery town on the Mexican border. It’s the cowboy boot capital of the world, and people come from everywhere to get the famous handmade boots with silver spurs.

You go to one of the local diners to sample a local dish. You settle on very spicy chili. You take a bite and hope that you’ll be able to talk when you're done. You check out your voice on the waitress; it's a little croaky after all that hot food, but she can understand you.

"Yes, I saw the man you're after," she tells you. "I recall he said something about going to a place with space in its name. But it's so busy here, I didn't have much time to talk to him." Then the waitress goes off to tend to a customer. Hmmm, not much time to talk to you, either!

You check out the clues as you head back to San Antonio, Texas (34).

103. You're in a small house in downtown Helena, Montana, but there's no sign of Earl E. Bird. Finally you admit defeat and head for 120.

104. You've arrived in Madison, Wisconsin, but there's nothing much for you here. You go to the local office, and the secretary hands you a postcard. It's from the Chief, and it tells you to shoot right over to 31.

105. As you drive into Sequioa National Park, in California, you wonder what a sequioa is. You soon discover that it is a kind of tree — one of the largest and oldest kinds on the face of the earth. The largest sequoia is the General Sherman Tree, which is 36 feet wide at its base and 272 feet tall.

The park ranger tells you that the tree is thought to be over three and a half-thousand years old and that it weighs over two thousand tons. That's some tree!

You ask about the thief you're tracking, and if the ranger saw her.

"She didn't seem too impressed by our trees," he admits. "She said they should chop them down and build houses from them. What an attitude! Anyway, she said she was off to look for a crop that's always made into something useful — corn."

You thank him and head back to San Francisco, California (65), to jot down the clues.

106. Fort Laramie, Wyoming, used to be an important post for the U.S. Cavalry. You're surprised to find that it's been restored to how it used to look in the last century, when the cavalry rode all over Wyoming to protect the settlers.

You ask one of the "soldiers" on duty about the thief you're after.

"Yes, I saw him," the man tells you. "He said this place was depressing and that he was heading to a place where he could see corn."

You thank him for his help and head back to Cheyenne, Wyoming (163), to check your clues.

107. As you arrive in Waco, Texas, you note that this is where the soft drink Dr Pepper was first made. You order one in the local cafe while you check out the rest of your information.

There's a Texas Rangers museum in town, and a riverboat, the *Brazos Queen*, makes trips down the Brazos River. But you don't have time for a ride. You note that Baylor University has a famous medical school in town, and on a hunch, you check it out.

"Yes, the man you're after was here," the doctor tells you. "He was suffering from a stomachache after eating too much fried chicken. I gave him some medicine and sent him packing. He muttered something about going where there's a lot of timber."

Heading back to Austin, Texas (119), you try to figure out the clues you've been given.

108. You've arrived in Raleigh, North Carolina. It's a pretty town with a lot of fine buildings and statues, including one that commemorates the two presidents born in North Carolina: Andrew Johnson and James Polk.

The local agent meets you and hands you a sheet of paper. "Here you are," she tells you. "Three places that the thief visited and three towns that she might have gone on to from here. Have fun."

"Oh, sure I will," you tell her. "I just love running from one end of the country to the other. It's very educational."

If you want to look into:
Roanoke, North Carolina —go to 27
Asheville, North Carolina —go to 80
Kitty Hawk, North Carolina —go to 11

If you've tracked the thief to:
Madison, Wisconsin —go to 104
Atlanta, Georgia —go to 129
Sacramento, California —go to 56

109. Carson City, Nevada, is the gateway to a large area of desert where nothing seems to grow. That just about describes your hopes of being on the right track. You realize there's no one here to meet you. With a sinking feeling, you head off to 31.

110. You're now in Little Rock, Arkansas. You're also truly on your own. There's no sign of the local agent. When you call the office, they tell you he's gone to 31. You head there right away.

111. The Craters of the Moon National Monument, in Idaho, is a fascinating place to visit. It has all the remains of volcanic activity —

craters and lava flow. You think to yourself just how much the place really does look like the moon.

It's a strange place, just the sort of spot one of Carmen's weird gang members might like. You wonder if they call the local guides astronauts.

Stopping to talk to one of the guides, you ask about the man you're after.

The guide remembers seeing him. "He didn't like the look of this place. I recall he mentioned wanting to go bird-watching next. Some bird with a one-word name, that's all I know."

You head back to Earth — er, Boise, Idaho (55), and add up your clues.

112. You're in Boise, Idaho — but soon it's quite obvious that you shouldn't be. You call your office, and your secretary tells you to head for 31 as fast as you can.

113. You've tracked Molly Coddle to a small park in Atlanta, Georgia. Taped to one of the swings, is a message with your name on it. It reads: Go to 120.

114. You're in Keokuk, Iowa. You read that Mark Twain once worked here for a short while, and that the town has the only existing oil portrait of the famous author.

Your trail leads you to Keokuk Dam, which

contains the largest dam locks on the upper Mississippi River. It also has no less than 119 spillways. An impressive dam!

You speak to the lockkeeper about the thief, and he bursts out laughing.

"Sure I remember him," he tells you. "Black-haired fella, a bit crazy. He thought I was an expert in *jail locks*. What a nut! When he discovered his mistake he told me he was going to a museum of transportation — probably looking for something to make a getaway in!"

You both have another good laugh. You thank him and head back to Des Moines, Iowa (1), to check out the clues he gave you.

115. You arrive in Lake Havasu City, Arizona. You're surprised to see old London Bridge. You ask one of the salesgirls in the English village why the bridge is there. She explains that it was shipped over in pieces from London and reassembled as a tourist attraction.

"Actually," she adds, "the people who bought it thought they were buying Tower Bridge, but this one is just as good."

You agree with her about that. Then you mention the crook you're after.

"He was here," she says. "But I didn't get to talk to him. The police chased him out of town."

Well, aside from seeing the bridge, this was a waste of time. Back to Flagstaff, Arizona (140).

116. You're up in the mountains, on the hunt for Miles Long, but you might as well be on the moon. There's no sign of him at all, so you pack up and head straight for 120.

117. Just outside of Tucson, Arizona, is Old Tucson, which is not really an old town at all but a movie lot that only *looks* like an Old West town. Many films and television shows have been shot here, and it's something of a tourist attraction. You find one of the movie "cowboys" and chat with him.

"Yeah, I saw that woman you're after. She didn't stay long, but before she left, she said she was going to a place where she could watch wheat grow. A strange lady, if you ask me."

You agree with him completely and write down the clue. Then you head back to Phoenix, Arizona (85).

118. You arrive in a small ghost town and instantly know it's the right place. On the town's horizon is the Alamo! You quietly creep into the old buildings and hunt for Nick Brunch. You find him in the old saloon, sipping a soda and gloating to himself.

"First I'll get this town back into shape." (*You can't believe he's sitting there laughing to himself!)* "Then I'll arrange for a big advertising campaign: *'Remember the Alamo!'* Yes, that's catchy! Hoo boy! I'm going to get rich with my Old West Theme Park!"

"I have a better idea," you call out. "Why not start a theme park in jail. You can call it 'Prison World.'"

The police arrive and take Nick into custody. You call the Chief. He congratulates you, tells you to come in and pick up your vacation tickets, and reminds you to check the scoring chart in the back of the book to see if you earned a promotion.

119. You've arrived in Austin, Texas. Texas is a big state — the second largest state, after Alaska. You know there's a lot of ground to cover if the local agent hasn't done his work. You give a sigh of relief when he shows up. He's brought you a car from the office and a sheet of paper. On the paper are places where the crook has been sighted and the possible towns he may have gone to.

If you want to check out:

Waco, Texas — go to 107

The Lyndon B. Johnson Space Center, in Houston, Texas—go to 22

Amarillo, Texas — go to 164

If you're ready to move on, then for:
Helena, Montana — go to 132
Cheyenne, Wyoming — go to 75
Little Rock, Arkansas — go to 39

120. Well, you've tracked the thief to the right town — but you've added up your clues incorrectly and you've tried to arrest the wrong person. Acme can get sued for this kind of thing. Better go to the scoring chart at the back of the book and see what the damage has been. Please be more careful in the future and, oh yes, add ten travel points to your score.

121. You are beginning to like Camden, Maine, now that you've discovered that the Camden River runs beneath the main street. It becomes a glittering waterfall before it finally enters the sea. You look out over the water and see dozens of small islands. It's really a great view, and you wish you had more time to enjoy it. But for now it's back to work.

Entering an office where you can book a ride on a tall, sail-powered schooner, you ask the person there about the woman you're tracking.

"She was here a while ago," the girl tells you. "But she suddenly remembered that she gets seasick easily, and changed her mind about the trip.

She said she was going to look for some electronics instead. Oh, yes, I also remember she had brown hair."

You add the clues to your notes as you head back to Rockland, Maine (100).

122. You step off the plane in Atlanta, Georgia. It's an impressive, sprawling, modern city. You like the place immediately, and the local agent is just as bright, efficient, and cheerful as the city seems to be.

"I've found three places that the thief visited," she tells you, handing you a list. "But rumor has it that more of Carmen's gang are in town."

"More for us to lock up, to make the streets safer for honest citizens," you tell her.

You look at the list. There's not much to go on, but with a little luck, it'll be enough.

If you want to look into:

Jekyll Island, Georgia — go to 81

Pine Mountain, Georgia — go to 138

Fernbank Science Center, in Atlanta, Georgia — go to 53

123. You turn off I-80 at Reno, Nevada, and take the final stretch of road down to Lake Tahoe and Carson City. It's been a long drive through Nevada, with nothing much to see except sun and

sand. Lake Tahoe appears before you and it looks cool and inviting, but you settle for a cold drink while meeting with the local agent.

"Not much to go on," he admits. "There's been trouble. Some of Carmen's gang drifted into town, and they're all kinda itchy on their trigger fingers, if ya know what I mean."

You do indeed; it means that you must be getting close to the thief. It's always a good sign when there's trouble in town — it drags the rats out into the daylight so you can catch them.

"Your thief's dressed like a modern-day cowboy, with a huge Stetson hat, high-heeled boots, and a thick leather belt." Grinning, he hands you a list. The list is short, but it's enough for you.

If you want to investigate:

The Nevada ghost town — go to 25

Glitter Gulch, Las Vegas, Nevada — go to 94

Death Valley, Nevada — go to 131

124. From Bayfield, Wisconsin, you board a ferry that sets off across Lake Superior to the Apostle Islands. There are twenty-two islands, most of which are scenic nature reserves used only in summer. But one of the islands, Madeline, has year-round resident.

When the ferry docks, you talk to one of the island locals and ask her about the thief.

"Yes, I remember him," she tells you. "A blue-eyed fellow. Seemed a bit upset when he arrived here, and he left soon after. Said he was going to look for some textiles."

You thank her for her help and take the ferry back to the mainland. Making a note of her clues, you return to Madison, Wisconsin (99).

125. You've finally arrived in Carson City, Nevada. But when you arrive, there's no one to meet you. When you check in with the local office, they tell you to go immediately to 31.

126. You find Dazzle Annie Nonker in Atlanta, Georgia, at the Federal Reserve Building, which also houses a bank museum.

You're sure Annie's here to commit another robbery. Sure enough, she's inside with an odd-looking machine gun. Instead of bullets, it shoots glue! She's already stuck the guards and tellers together in a giant glob of glue. None of them can reach their guns or sound the alarm buttons.

"Ha!" She laughs. "I love a good stick-up!" Whistling happily, she starts to load the cash from the drawers into her huge handbag.

Time to catch her. But how can you avoid getting all gummed up? Suddenly you have an idea. You sneak out to a hardware store down the street and buy a paint gun and a gallon of fast-drying red paint. Now you're ready for action. When you return to the bank, Annie is still cleaning out the cash.

"Hold it, Annie!" you call.

She doesn't, of course. Instead, she goes for her gun. You're faster than she is, though, and you shoot her with a spray of red paint. Soon she's as stiff as a board from the neck down, and wrapped in a cocoon of redness.

"Caught you red-handed," you tell her. When the police arrive, they have to pick Annie up and carry her out. "I'm sure the judge will give you a stiff sentence," you call out to her, laughing.

The police tell you that they've recovered the Golden Gate Bridge. Cheerfully you call up the Chief to pass on the good news.

"Well done," he tells you. "Those tickets for Hawaii are all ready for you, along with a good bonus for solving the case. Head for the scoring chart at the back of the book to see if you've won yourself a promotion!"

127. You're in Madison, Wisconsin, and you look around. It's a nice town, but why isn't someone here to greet you? You check in at the local office, and they're real surprised to see you. No one told them you were coming, and none of

Carmen's gang has been seen here for years. They suggest you try 31.

128. You find yourself at a deserted fairground. Seems like an odd place for one of Carmen's gang to hide out. Sure enough, you're looking in the wrong place. It's time to head for 120.

129. You're in Atlanta, Georgia, but its fabled Southern hospitality doesn't seem to be awaiting you. When you call the local office, they tell you that you've come to the wrong place and that you should head immediately for 31.

130. Carson City, Nevada — near the shores of beautiful Lake Tahoe. Sadly, you discover that this is the wrong place for you right now. Sighing, you head for 31.

131. Death Valley, Nevada, is legendary for its heat. In 1913 the highest temperature ever recorded in the United States was measured here at 134° Fahrenheit. You're glad it's not that hot right now. You head down to Badwater, the heart of the valley. It's 282 feet below sea level. When you arrive, you find a grizzled old prospector.

You ask him about the man you're after. He

thinks for a moment and then tries to hit you with the bucket he's carrying. Oh, no, one of Carmen's agents! You grab the bucket and wrestle it from his hand. Then you slam it over his head.

"You look a little *pail*, pal. Must be the heat. I'll have the police lock you up in a nice cell where you can cool your heels!"

Obviously, you're getting very close. Time to return to Carson City, Nevada (123).

132. You've arrived in Helena, Montana. The city was founded in 1864 when a group of discouraged miners decided to try one last time to look for gold. They struck it rich. You only hope you'll be as lucky in catching the man you're after.

The local agent arrives and shakes your hand warmly. "Here you go," he tells you. "It's not much, but it should be of some help. And I have to tell you that some of Carmen's agents are in town." You thank him and look over his list.

If you want to check out:

Charles Russell's studio, in Great Falls, Montana —go to 51

Butte, Montana —go to 144

The Custer Battlefield in Montana —go to 91

133. You've reached Cincinnati, Ohio, a city with much to offer residents and visitors. There are fine museums, beautiful gardens, and even summer riverboat cruises that go as far as New Orleans. But no time for that now. You head for the Taft Museum, which houses a priceless collection of portraits, architecture, jewelry, and porcelain. It would make a terrific haul for any of Carmen's gang, and you're certain that the thief you're after must have been here.

Your hunch is correct. You talk to a museum guard who remembers the woman you're after. "I heard her say she was going to look for soybeans after this."

Okay! You're onto something, so it's back to Columbus, Ohio (137), to investigate more clues.

134. So this is Cheyenne, Wyoming. It's a pretty enough town, but there's nothing here for you. Better head to 31.

135. You've reached Atlanta, Georgia, and the local agent isn't here to greet you. You wait impatiently, but there's still no sign of her. Finally you call the local office. The person who answers is surprised to hear from you.

"I was told you were going to 31," she explains. "Maybe you'd better head there right now."

136. You've driven into Cheyenne, Wyoming. Once this was a wild town, with gunfights in the streets and bad men everywhere. Now it seems very quiet. Too quiet, in fact. You check in with the local office, and they tell you to go to 31.

137. Columbus, Ohio, is a delightful town with lots to offer — if you had the time to spend, but you don't. You head for your meeting spot with the local agent. He's picked an appropriate spot — the local

branch of the Ohio State Library. With almost a million books in its collection, there's plenty of information on hand!

The agent has information that you can use, too. He gives you his list, and you look it over.

If you want to investigate:

Cleveland, Ohio, Metroparks Zoo — go to 40
The Air Force Museum, in Ohio — go to 19
Cincinnati, Ohio — go to 133

If you're ready to move on to:

Little Rock, Arkansas — go to 72
Atlanta, Georgia — go to 149
Raleigh, North Carolina — go to 108

138. Pine Mountain, Georgia, was once the second home of the 32nd president of the United States, Franklin Delano Roosevelt, and he died here in 1945. His house was called the Little White House, and it has been preserved in memory of him. Roosevelt loved the peaceful atmosphere at Pine Mountain, but that's not what you find right now.

As you get out of your car, an arrow zips past your ear. Startled, you dive for cover. You can see a man with a crossbow running toward you and loading another bolt into the bow. A regular William Tell, this guy!

Thinking fast, you search your pockets for something to use against him. All you've got is the apple you didn't eat for lunch. It will have to do. When he's close enough, you stand up and throw the apple as hard as you can.

You've caught the assassin by surprise. He shoots at the apple but misses, and it hits him full in the face. Before he can recover, you jump him. One quick karate chop and he's weaponless.

"Okay, Tell, tell me what you know. Where's Carmen's gang hiding out?"

If you're after:

Molly Coddle — go to 113
June Bug — go to 146
Earl E. Bird — go to 28
Mylar Naugahyde — go to 61
Miles Long — go to 4
Polly Esther Fabrique — go to 162
Dazzle Annie Nonker — go to 126
Nick Brunch — go to 97

139. You go to the address you have for Earl E. Bird. It's a hotel called the Flamingo Hilton. Figures — a bird address. You check the place out, but there's no bird to be seen. A messenger hands you a slip of paper that reads: Go to 120.

140. You've landed in Flagstaff, Arizona. It's

very close to Grand Canyon National Park. When you arrive at the park, you talk to the rangers who are looking after the mules that take tourists down into the canyon. Now, thanks to the thief, the mules have nothing to go down into.

"When the thief stole the Grand Canyon," the head ranger tells you, "he dropped a sheet of paper. We believe it contains three possible places the thief plans to visit in Arizona, and three possible destinations the thief might escape to in another part of the country."

If you want to check out:
The Petrified Forest, in Arizona — go to 26
London Bridge, in Arizona — go to 115
Tombstone, Arizona — go to 87

If you think the thief has gone to:
Raleigh, North Carolina — go to 2
Phoenix, Arizona — go to 156
Boise, Idaho — go to 55

141. You arrive at the I.Q. Zoo in Hot Springs, Arkansas, on the trail of Nick Brunch. The zoo features performances by trained animals, but there's no sign of Brunch. Suspecting that the animals have more intelligence than you do, you pack up and head for 120.

142. The Salisbury House, in Iowa, is actually a replica of a sixteenth-century home from Salisbury, England. It was built by a Des Moines millionaire who was a direct descendant of the sixteenth-century town's mayor. Looking around the museum, you can see why one of Carmen's gang would be interested in the place. It is filled with authentic (not to mention valuable) Tudor furnishing from Olde England.

You talk to the guide, and she recalls seeing the woman you're after. "Blond-haired," she says. "She mentioned that next she was going to a place where there was plenty of timber."

You thank her and head back to Des Moines, Iowa, (37), to check out more clues.

143. Abilene, Texas, was once a legendary frontier town where the cattle trails ended and the cattle were shipped out by railroad. It's not as dusty and wild nowadays — there're very few cowboys celebrating the end of a cattle drive. You do find a local cowgirl, though, who saw the man you're after.

"He said he was going somewhere that had something to do with space," the cowgirl tells you.

You head back to San Antonio, Texas (34), to check out where this could be.

144. Butte, Montana, is an old mining town, first settled in 1864. People dug up gold and silver here, but the real fortune is in copper — over seventeen billion dollars' worth. You can see why Carmen's gang is interested in the place.

You go into one of the supply shops to check leads. You ask the owner about the thief you're hunting, and you notice a man who is glancing around.

"Look out!" the shopkeeper yells. You spin around just in time to see the man coming at you with a pickax! You jump to one side and grab his arm. With a quick judo flip, you throw him into the vegetable bin.

"Tossed salad," you mutter as you pull him out. He struggles to punch you, but you dodge his blow and and hit him hard. He collapses into a pile of electric bulbs. "Lights out," you add.

The owner calls the police. It's obvious you're getting very close to the culprit now! Go back to Helena, Montana (132) — but beware — Carmen's gang is also on your trail!

145. You enter Hancock Park, in California, to find the La Brea Tar Pits museum. From around 3 million B.C. (up to 10,000 B.C.) the La Brea Tar Pits were a sticky bog that trapped many animals. The remains of these animals

were preserved in the bog, and scientists have found some terrific examples of saber-toothed tigers and mammoths.

Though you'd love to take a closer look, you know you'd be stuck there for hours. With a sigh, you talk to the woman at the entrance.

She saw the woman you're after. "She said these animals were too sticky and icky for her. She mentioned going to look for mockingbirds."

You thank her and head back to Sacramento, California (56). You make one note of the clue and another note reminding you to return to the pits when you have more time.

146. You've tracked June Bug to the fascinating Toy Museum in Atlanta, Georgia. But though there're plenty of things here to attract your attention, none of them include June Bug. Realizing you're on the wrong track, you head for 120.

147. You've arrived in Boise, Idaho. It's probably the potato capital of the world, but you're not interested in getting any food. After a few hours, you realize that you're in the wrong place and have to head to 31.

148. This is Augusta, Maine. It's a terrific

place to have fresh lobsters. But they aren't on your menu right now. Instead, you must go to 31.

149. Atlanta, Georgia, is a delightful town, even if it's a bit too hot and humid right now. But the real problem may be that you're hot under the collar after discovering that there's no one here to meet you. You head off to 31.

150. Sheridan, Wyoming, is a relic of the Wild West and the gateway to the Bighorn Mountains. Every year there's a rodeo here. You'd love to stay and catch it, but the only thing you have time to catch now is a crook. You talk to one of the rodeo workers, and he remembers seeing the woman you're after.

"She had the prettiest green eyes I ever did see." He sighs. "I asked her to brand a few steers with me, but she said she had to get some peanuts."

"Shame on you," you tell him. But at least you've gotten two clues. You head back to Cheyenne, Wyoming (158), to check on your next destination.

151. When you arrive in Rockland, Maine, the Maine Seafoods Festival is in full swing. There are so many delicious-looking dishes to sample, you wish you could spend a few days here.

Shrimp, lobster, fish . . . Your mouth is watering, but you steel yourself. You go over and talk to one of the shopkeepers, who remembers the man you're hunting.

"Yes, he told me he loved water," the shopkeeper says. "In fact, he said he was off to see a famous lake after he'd sampled some of the food here."

"Nice to see he had the time," you growl. "I'll just take a cup of clam chowder — to go." You eat your soup as you head back to Augusta, Maine (74), to follow up this lead.

152. You've tracked Mylar Nauguhyde to Avalanche Basin, in Montana. He must like scenic wonders! This is a valley with walls two thousand feet high and waterfalls that cascade over them. Red cedars are all around you. It's a very pretty sight, and suddenly you see something that's even more welcome to your eyes. It's Mylar, staring at the waterfalls.

"Give up, Mylar, there's nowhere to hide!"

He tries to make a break for it, but you're too quick for him. A fast football tackle, low down on his legs, sends him tumbling.

"I'm taking you in, Mylar. Come clean and tell me where you've hidden the Grand Canyon." He points to the canyon in a corner of the valley.

After you hand Mylar over to the police, you call the Chief to tell him that you've accomplished your mission. He's thrilled and promises to have your Hawaii tickets waiting. In the meantime, he suggests you go to the chart at the back of the book to check your score!

153. Eureka Springs, Arkansas, is a very strange place. It's built on the side of a blasted-out mountain. The town has many levels and long, winding streets. Some of the buildings look as if they're leaning over. Maybe they don't like heights either.

You see that Carry Nation once lived here, and her house is now an exhibit. Nation was a staunch foe of alcohol and used a huge hatchet to smash up bars in the Old West. When you arrive at her house, there's a man waiting for you — holding a huge hatchet.

You've got a bad feeling about this. The man swings at you. You duck and plow into him instead. A quick karate chop to the neck knocks him out. Whew! That was close. And speaking of close, the villain you are after can't be far away now. Carefully, you head back to Little Rock, Arkansas (161).

154. You get off the plane in Atlanta, Georgia,

and hear yourself being paged. Going to the nearest phone, you identify yourself, and hear the Chief on the other end.

"What are you doing there?" he growls. "Go to 31 immediately!"

155. You stop at the doors of the Fabrique Boutique in Reno, Nevada. Can this really be where Polly Esther Fabrique is hiding? It seems a little too obvious. When you go in, you discover the store is only a dummy. Polly's not here. Discouraged, you head off to 120.

156. You've arrived in Phoenix, Arizona, but there's no local agent here to greet you. When you call the office, they tell you you're in the wrong place and should head directly to 31.

157. You've arrived at the Ozark Folk Center, at Mountain View, Arkansas, which celebrates the traditional folk music of the area. There's no celebrating for you, however. There isn't any sign of Dazzle Annie Nonker, so, with a sigh, you head for 120.

158. You get out of your car in Cheyenne, Wyoming. There's a parade under way, and the local agent calls you over.

"Am I that famous?" you ask him. "I've never had a parade in my honor before."

"Sorry, it's not for you, pardner," he answers. "You've arrived during the Cheyenne Days — a celebration of life that's held every July."

What a shame — it would have been nice to have been greeted like this! Instead, you settle for taking the list the agent has brought you.

If you want to investigate:
Yellowstone National Park, in Wyoming
— go to 45
Grand Teton National Park, in Wyoming
— go to 77
Sheridan, Wyoming — go to 150

If you're ready to move on to:
Carson City, Nevada — go to 109
Atlanta, Georgia — go to 122
Olympia, Washington — go to 24

159. Fort Dodge, Iowa, is a restored U.S. Cavalry outpost that was originally built in 1850. The old post office, hotel, and two cabins are actually the originals. You almost expect the Sixth Cavalry to ride past you and through the gates. Instead, you find one of the local guides, who's seen the crook you're after.

"Black-haired dude," he tells you. "He said this

place was too out-of-date for him, and that he was going where they made plenty of electronic equipment."

You thank him for his help and head back to Des Moines, Iowa (1), to put things together.

160. Little Rock, Arkansas, is in the State of Opportunity, but there're no opportunities here for you. The trail has run cold. Go to 31.

161. You've arrived in Little Rock, Arkansas. It's an old city founded around 1821 and still has many of the fine old buildings from its historic past. You go to the oldest building in town, the Hinderliter House, an authentic log cabin — to meet the local agent.

She's there with a list for you. "Took some hard work," she tells you. "Carmen's gang seems out in full force, and I had to arrest two people before I could finish and meet you."

You congratulate her on her work and study the information she's gathered.

If you want to look into:

The Crater of Diamonds, Arkansas — go to 7
Eureka Springs, Arkansas — go to 153
Grand Prarie, Arkansas — go to 96

162. You've arrived at Fort King George in

Darien. This was the first settlement in Georgia, but it might as well be on the moon as far as you're concerned. There's no sign of Polly Esther Fabrique, so you head off to 120.

163. You've arrived in Cheyenne, Wyoming. This Old West town is now very modern and clean, and you like it immediately. You also like the local agent, who arrives with a sheet of paper for you.

"I've found three places where your thief was spotted and three towns he may be heading for," he tells you.

If you want to investigate:
Devils Tower, Wyoming — go to 29
Fort Laramie, Wyoming — go to 106
Cody, Wyoming — go to 90

If you're ready to travel to:
Des Moines, Iowa — go to 1
Madison, Wisconsin — go to 62
Boise, Idaho — go to 147

164. Amarillo, Texas, bills itself as the "helium capital of the world." You stop at the Helium Monument, where a number of time capsules have been buried, and talk to the monument ticket seller. She remembers seeing the man you're

trailing and recalls that he mentioned going on to a famous battle site.

You head back to Austin, Texas (119), and make a note of this information.

165. You've trailed Molly Coddle to the Central Mall in Fort Smith, Arkansas, but there's no sign of her in all the shops here. You finally realize that you have to go to 120.

166. You're in Little Rock, Arkansas, but after a short wait you realize that you shouldn't be. You take the trail out to 31 instead.

167. Dallas, Texas, is a huge sprawling town. You wonder if you'll be able to spot J. R. Ewing here, let alone your thief. Actually, Dallas is teamed with Fort Worth, since the two cities have grown together. The combination has produced one of the country's largest convention and business areas. You wonder what funny business Carmen's gang is trying to pull here. You stop to talk to the local police chief.

"Yeah, that thief was spotted by a couple of people. One of them said that the man was going to a state that had a bird for a mascot, and that the bird had a color in its name."

Heading back to San Antonio, Texas (34), you

check this against your own information.

168. Milwaukee, Wisconsin, is one of the most beautiful old towns in America. When you see the lovely buildings by the shore of Lake Michigan, you're inclined to agree. It's a short drive to the old public library, one of the nicest buildings in the city.

You ask the head librarian about the man you're hunting.

"He was here and he tried to steal some books! Can you imagine! The librarian who saw him said he had blue eyes and tried to steal books about peanuts."

You thank her and head back to Madison, Wisconsin (99), to check out the clues.

169. Raleigh, North Carolina, is named for a famous English explorer — but you'll be remembered only for following the wrong trail. Head for 31 right away.

170. Atlanta, Georgia, is a nice place to be — if you're supposed to be there. You aren't, and you have to pack up everything and head for 31.

SCORING CHART

Add up all of your travel points (you did remember to mark one point for each time you moved to a new number, didn't you?). If you have penalty points for trying to arrest the wrong person, add those in, too. Then check your score against the chart below to see how you did.

0 – 17: You couldn't really have solved these cases in these few steps. Either you're boasting about your abilities or you're actually working with Carmen's gang. Be honest and try again —if you dare!

18 – 40: Super sleuth! You work very well and don't waste time. Well done — you deserve the new rank and the nice big bonus you'll get next payday!

41 – 60: Private eye material! You're a good, steady worker, and you get your man (or woman). Still, there's room for improvement, and you can always try again to get another promotion.

61 – 80: Detective first class. You're not a world-famous private eye yet, but you're getting there. Try again and see if you can move up a grade or two!

81 – 100: Rookie material. You're taking too long to track down the crooks. Next time they're going to get away from you. Try a little harder and see if you're really better than this.

Over 100: Are you sure you're really cut out to be a detective? Maybe you'd be better off looking for an easier job — a janitor for Acme, maybe? Still, if you're determined to be a detective, why not try again and see if this was just an off day. Better luck next time!